This well-known fairytale is delightfully illustrated and simply retold to entertain all young listeners.

Titles in Series S852
Cinderella
Three Little Pigs
Goldilocks and the Three Bears
Jack and the beanstalk
Snow White and the Seven Dwarfs
These titles are also available as a Gift Box set

British Library Cataloguing in Publication Data
Murdock, Hy
  Snow White and the seven dwarfs. — (Fairy tales. Series 852; 5)
  I. Title   II. Grundy, Lynn N.   III. Series
  823'.914[J]   PZ8
  ISBN 0-7214-9530-3

First Edition

© LADYBIRD BOOKS LTD MCMLXXXV
© Illustrations LYNN N GRUNDY MCMLXXXV

Snow White and the Seven Dwarfs

written by HY MURDOCK

illustrated by LYNN N GRUNDY

Ladybird Books Loughborough

Once upon a time, there was a wicked Queen. She had a magic mirror and often she would stand in front of it and say, 'Mirror, Mirror on the wall, who is the fairest of us all?' And the magic mirror always said,

You, O Queen, are the fairest of us all.

Now the King had a little girl called Snow White. Snow White was very pretty. She had skin as white as snow, with rosy red cheeks and black hair. As she grew up, she became more and more beautiful.

One day, when the wicked Queen asked
the mirror, 'Who is the fairest of us all?'
it said,
Queen, you are fairer than most,
  it is true,
But Snow White is fairer still than you.

This made the Queen jealous and she became very angry. She called for a huntsman and told him to take Snow White into the forest and kill her.

The man was sad. He loved Snow White and so he didn't kill her but just left her in the forest.

Snow White wandered along until she came to a tiny little cottage. When she went inside, she found a small table and

seven tiny chairs and seven little beds.
She lay down on the seventh bed and
went to sleep.

The cottage was the home of seven
dwarfs. Each day they went to work in
a mine, digging for gold. When they got
home that night, they found Snow
White.

She told the dwarfs what had happened and they asked Snow White to stay with them. For a long time they were all very happy.

Then one day, the wicked Queen spoke to her magic mirror again. 'Mirror, Mirror on the wall, who is the fairest of us all?' And the mirror said,

Queen, you are fairer than most,
it is true,
But Snow White is fairer still than you.

The Queen knew now that the huntsman had tricked her. The mirror told her that Snow White was alive and well and staying with the seven dwarfs.

So the wicked Queen put some poison in a shiny red apple. Then she dressed up as an old woman and set off over the hills and into the forest to find the seven dwarfs' cottage.

The Queen found Snow White and gave her the poisoned apple. The girl didn't know that the old woman was really the wicked Queen.

Snow White bit into the apple. But the next moment, she fell to the ground. She lay there until the dwarfs found her. They all thought that she was dead.

The dwarfs guessed that the wicked Queen had done this. They were very sad, for they had all loved Snow White.

They put her in a glass case and set it
on the hill so that they could always
see her.

And so for many years, Snow White lay in the glass case. It seemed as though she was asleep and she looked as beautiful as ever. One of the dwarfs was always there to watch over her.

One day a handsome prince rode by. He saw Snow White and loved her straight away. He asked the dwarfs if he could take her in the glass case and look after her himself.

But then, as they moved Snow White,
the piece of poisoned apple fell from her
mouth and she awoke. She was alive
and well once more.

The prince asked Snow White to marry him. He told her that he would make sure that the wicked Queen never harmed her again. And so the prince, Snow White and the seven dwarfs all lived happily ever after.